The Midnight Teenager

Written by Lotachi Opara
Illustrated by Seun Ayanlowa

PUBLISHED BY
KRATOS PUBLISHERS

The Midnight Teenager
Copyright © 2024 by Lotachi Opara
Illustrations Copyright © 2024 by Seun Ayanlowa
Published by: Kratos Publisher

All rights reserved under international copyright law. No part of this book may be reproduced without permission in writing from the copyright owner, except by a reviewer, who may quote brief passages in review.

Contents

Chapter 1: The First Day of School	1
Chapter 2: History in the Making	6
Chapter 3: A Dangerous Discussion	11
Chapter 4: A Big Mistake	15
Chapter 5: Rescue Mission	19
Chapter 6: The Cave	25
Chapter 7: Revenge	35
Chapter 8: Home Time	39

Chapter One

The First Day of School

Beep. Beep. Beep.

Mya shut her alarm clock off, bolting upright in bed in shock. It was seven o'clock in the morning. She hadn't gotten up this early all summer.

The First Day of School

"Mya, wake up! We're going to be late for the first day of school," shouted Mya's little brother Henry, appearing at her bedroom door.

"I'm awake," she grumbled, rubbing her eyes. "Go and get dressed."

Their mum and dad had already left for work, so once they were dressed and had eaten breakfast, Mya and Henry walked to school together.

When they arrived at the school gate, Henry suddenly felt nervous.

"What if I don't make any friends?" He asked Mya. She smiled at him.

The First Day of School

"Of course you'll make friends! Everyone in Year Seven is brand new to the schoo-"

"Is that James?" Henry interrupted her.

Much to Mya's surprise, she looked up and saw that the boy walking towards them was, in fact, James. He and Mya had been best friends throughout primary school, but his parents moved cities afterwards. He had gone to a different secondary school, so they hadn't seen each other since the last day of Year Six. Today was the first day of Year Nine.

Still, Mya was happy to see him. As she caught James' eye, she smiled in a friendly way, and then saw the three boys behind him. Ben, Max, and Ryan: Year Nine's bullies.

Her face fell as she noticed them all laughing and messing around with James. Ryan had his arm around James' shoulder, and they were all shouting football chants.

"Hi, James! Do you remember me?" Henry beamed, running up to him. Mya hadn't noticed him bounding over.

"Henry!" She hissed at him, quickly walking up to them.

The First Day of School

The boys all turned to laugh at Henry, jeering at his too-big new school backpack and shiny black shoes. James looked up.

"Hi, Mya," he said, raising an eyebrow at her menacingly. "Did you miss me?"

Chapter Two

History in the Making

"Class, settle down now!" instructed Mr. Williams' booming voice. "Who can tell me who built the first sailing boat in ancient history?"

"Oh, me!" Someone shouted out.

Mya didn't listen to the answer. She had Science, Maths, and now History – her least favourite subject – with James. In Science, he had been sitting with Ben and Max, and they had set fire to another boy's tie with the Bunsen burner. In Maths, he and Ryan got sent out for throwing things across the classroom. Now, in History, Mr. Williams had seated James next to her.

She had been beyond excited to catch up with him when she first saw him, but now she was scared. He was different now; he was turning into a bully, just like his new friends.

"Are you not going to talk to me?" James nudged her elbow. They'd barely spoken all lesson. She'd found out they moved back for James' dad's new job, but she didn't know else what to say to him.

There was a whack on the back of her head, and a ball of paper dropped to the floor. She turned around and saw Ben, Max and Ryan laughing. James was snickering beside her.

"Why are you friends with them?" Mya muttered.

"We met over the summer when I rejoined the local football club," James replied. "They're funny. They're only having a laugh."

"No, they're not funny," snapped Mya. "They're horrible, and you're turning horrible too."

The bell sounded for the end of the lesson.

Mya grabbed her bag and went to storm out of the classroom when James suddenly shouted behind her.

"Mya, stop!"

He caught up with her, blocking her exit.

"I'm not horrible, I promise. Let me prove it to you. Meet me tonight in the park behind Redbridge Library like we used to," he said.

Mya thought about it. She did want to catch up with him, and she often hung out there after school anyway, listening to music. Maybe he was still the same.

"Please?" James added.

"Okay, sure," she replied.

Chapter 3

A Dangerous Discussion

Henry's last class of the day was about to start, and he was queueing up for the lesson when he heard a familiar voice behind him.

"That'll show her. Thinks she's better than me now, ha!" James laughed.

"We're so going to ruin her," replied Ben, giving James a high-five.

"Mya is going to be the biggest loser in Year Nine by the end of today," said Ryan.

Henry gasped and turned round, but the boys had already gone into their lesson. He needed to tell Mya what they said. He didn't know what they were planning, but it didn't sound good.

When the end of the school day came, Henry rushed out to where Mya was waiting for him.

"Ben said that he and Max and Ryan and James are going to ruin you, and Ryan said you're going to be the biggest loser in Year Nine by the end of today!" He yelled out, panting.

"What are you on about?" Mya asked, bewildered. Just then, James walked past them on his way out of the school gates.

A Dangerous Discussion

"See you later!" He called out to Mya with a wave.

"Don't go!" Henry begged her. "Something bad is going to happen."

"Nothing bad is going to happen, Henry," Mya replied. "I'm just meeting James to hang out and catch up for a bit."

A Dangerous Discussion

"Then, let me go with you!" Henry persisted.

"Not today. Come on, let's get home," Mya responded, sighing.

"Fine," said Henry, worried. He decided he'd have to take matters into his own hands.

Chapter 4

A Big Mistake

Mya waited until it was dark out and snuck out of the house through the back door. It was a short walk to the park, and she knew it well. She often hung out there by herself after school and listened to music.

A Big Mistake

When she reached the wall behind the library, she couldn't see James anywhere.

"James?" She whispered. There was a rustling behind her, and as she turned, she saw James emerge from the trees- shortly followed by Ben, Max and Ryan.

"What's going o-" she began, but Ryan lunged forward and grabbed her. Ben clamped some cloth over her mouth, and before she could react, the world went dizzy, and she felt herself slump to the ground.

A Big Mistake

When she woke up, she found herself in a big, deep hole with her mouth, arms and legs tied up. She looked up and saw James and his friends

A Big Mistake

surrounding her, but when she blinked and looked again, no one was there.

Chapter 5

Rescue Mission

Mya came around again, and despite the pitch-dark night, she noticed that she was in the middle of the woods and realised again that she was tied up everywhere. Even her mouth was covered, so she couldn't scream for help or climb out of the deep hole.

She didn't know what to do, and the panic was setting in. Suddenly, she heard footsteps and held her breath, expecting to see the boys peering down at her again.

To her surprise, a large robot wheeled itself up to the edge of the hole and began beeping loudly. It was joined by a figure. Mya realised the figure was a teenager, just like her.

"Hello, my name is Zack," the boy shouted down. Do you need some help?"

"Mhm!" Mya mumbled through the cloth her mouth was covered with, as loud as she could.

Zack jumped down into the hole and began untying her.

"Thank you," she said, "I'm Mya."

"What on earth happened here, Mya?" he replied.

She explained what James and his friends had done as Zack helped her climb out of the hole, and then the robot started beeping again.

"What is that thing?" she asked.

"This," Zack said proudly, pointing to his robot, "Is Z13. I've been building him for weeks, and I brought him out here to run some tests. He detects signs of life from up to fifteen metres away. That's how I found you."

"D'you reckon he could help us track down James? I'm not letting him get away with this."

So, Zack and Mya began their trek through the woods, led by Z13. He told her all about how he built the robot and the different things he could do, while Mya finished some leftover chips that Zack had brought along with him. She

Rescue Mission

was starving; she had no idea how long she'd been laying in that hole.

Suddenly, they reached a clearing in the woods and heard mumbling and banging.

"Z13, battle mode activate!" Zack instructed the robot.

The trio crept defensively towards the figure in the clearing, fully expecting to find the boys. Instead, Mya realised it was Henry, tied to a tree.

"What are you doing here?" She asked in shock, untying and hugging him, but she couldn't have been happier to see him.

"I came to rescue you!" He said, "But James and Max found me and tied me up."

Mya looked at Zack.

"Let's get them back," she said.

Chapter 6
The Cave

As they wandered through the dark woods, Mya wondered if they'd be better off going home and forgetting the whole thing. She couldn't understand why James had been so cruel to her, but she had never been so terrified in all her life, and she was scared that their revenge wouldn't go to plan.

The three of them were silent until they reached the middle of the woods. Henry began to whisper to himself, psyching himself up for if they came across the boys again. They reached a lake and heard whispers behind them. As soon as they turned around, James and his friends jumped out of the bushes again.

"Henry!" Mya shouted.

The boys grabbed Henry and were gone in the blink of an eye. Mya screamed, and Zack put a hand on her shoulder, pulling her back.

"We have to find my brother," she told him firmly, trying not to cry. "He came to try and save me all by himself."

Zack shifted awkwardly.

The Cave

"I need to go home, Mya. It's late, my Mum will be worrying about me. You should go home, too."

"I'm not leaving my brother here alone!"

Z13 beeped sadly, circling Zack's feet.

"I'm sorry," he said, "I can't stay here. I hope you find him."

Zack handed her a torch, then he and Z13 turned and left her in the forest. Mya couldn't bear the thought of leaving Henry alone, so she made a camp to stay overnight.

The Cave

As she lay there, she tried to work out where they ran off, but she couldn't remember. She hardly slept and was starving, but as the sun began to rise, she was determined to find Henry.

In the early hours of the morning, she set off.

The Cave

As she was wandering through the forest, she went along a river. She kept seeing shadows that looked just like Henry.

The Cave

"Mya!"

Someone in the distance shouted her name. Looking back, she saw a big cave at the end of the river. At the opening of the cave, she saw Henry being dragged inside by the boys.

Mya ran as fast as a cheetah but couldn't catch up. Henry had faded into the darkness as she reached the cave, but she began to make her way through it, flicking Zack's torch on to guide her. As she tread deeper and deeper into the cave, she lost her way and kept turning round and feeling like she'd gone in circles.

The cave walls began to narrow, and she saw three tunnels surrounding her. There was one going left, one going right and one in the middle.

Mya picked the middle, which strangely had graffiti all over the walls. She heard voices from deep inside the tunnel. Following the voices, she ventured as deep as she could and saw a big dark hole. As she got closer, she

The Cave

realised it was some kind of underground layer.

"Wow!" She breathed, momentarily distracted by the vastness of the cave.

As she moved inside the tunnel, she saw something. It was a graffiti picture of James. This cave must be the boys' hangout spot, she thought to herself, wondering if this was where they'd been all night.

As she got to the end of the path, she saw her little brother tied up against a large rock.

"Mya, you found me!" He sighed with relief. His face was wet with tears.

The Cave

Immediately, she untied the ropes that were attached to his legs and hands. They heard voices coming from further in the cave, coming closer.

"They're coming back," Mya whispered. "Come on, Henry, run!"

They began racing back through the cave, and behind them, they heard a huge bang that sounded like a bomb going off.

"Run all you like!" They heard one of the boys shout. "We'll still catch you!"

The boys' laughter echoed through the tunnels as Mya and Henry escaped.

The Cave

Chapter 7
Revenge

As Mya and Henry raced through the woods, the gang of trouble was right behind them, but eventually, they managed to lose them.

"Mya, look!" Henry said, pointing at a large ditch in the ground.

Revenge

They decided to make a trap to catch the boys. Mya was sure they deserved for her to get revenge now. They started building the trap with large leaves and twigs as quickly as possible. After a while of panicked foraging, building, and checking over their shoulders every few minutes in case the boys caught up to them, they finished their masterpiece.

There was rumbling coming up from behind them. Mya turned and saw James and his friends running towards them. Their eyes were like thunder roaring through the sky.

"You can't hide anymore!" James called out menacingly as he, Ben, Max, and Ryan hurtled towards them. They got almost close enough to grab them, and then suddenly Mya and her brother stood back, and James and his friends fell with a thud straight through their trap.

"Don't you ever, EVER, try and hurt me or my brother again!" Mya screamed at them.

Revenge

The pair watched as the boys grumbled and shouted, tripping over each other as they tried to climb out of the hole.

"You'll regret this!" James shouted back at Mya, but she and Henry turned and walked away, satisfied with their revenge.

Chapter 8

Home Time

"Where were you?!"

Mya and Henry's Mum pulled them into a huge hug and squeezed them tightly. The pair had gotten home safe and sound. Their Dad appeared from the kitchen, sighing in relief, "I'm so glad to see you."

"We were so worried about you." Their Mum whispered, planting kisses over their faces.

"I'm so glad to see you too!" Little Henry said, hugging his Mum hard.

"We were in a terrible and terrifying situation," said Mya.

"Let's make a cup of tea," Mum said, guiding Mya and Henry to sit down, "Then you can tell us all about it."

She went to make the tea as their Dad wrapped them in a warm blanket.

Home Time

As they sat there, Mya began to wonder whether her parents would even believe the story. If she hadn't been there, she wasn't sure she would believe it either. All she knew was that she was never going to let James and his friends, or anyone else for that matter, terrorise her or her brother ever again.

Her mind wandered to Zack and Z13. She didn't know where he had come from, or where he lived. She didn't know whether she'd ever see him again. All she had to remember this strange and frightening ordeal, and the mysterious midnight teenager who rescued her, were a few bruises and a battered old torch.

About the Author

Introducing Lotachi Opara (Lola), a vibrant and innovative young writer whose creativity knows no bounds. With a fresh perspective and a knack for storytelling, Lola captivates readers with her unique voice and imaginative narratives.

Born with a passion for words, Lola began crafting stories at a young age, weaving together worlds filled with wonder and intrigue. Her writing style is characterised by its vivid imagery, richly drawn characters, and thought-provoking themes that resonate with readers of all ages.

Drawing inspiration from a wide array of sources, from classic literature to contemporary culture, Lola infuses her work with a sense of vitality and originality. Whether exploring the depths of human emotion or venturing into the realms of fantasy and science fiction, she excels at creating immersive experiences that transport readers to new and exciting worlds.

Despite her youth, Lola has already made a significant impact on the literary scene, garnering critical acclaim and a devoted following. Her stories have been praised for their depth, complexity, and ability to provoke thought and inspire imagination.

With each new project, Lola continues to push the boundaries of storytelling, exploring new genres, experimenting with different narrative techniques, and challenging readers to see the world in a fresh and exciting way. With boundless creativity and a passion for storytelling, Lola is undoubtedly a rising star in the literary world, destined to leave a lasting impression on readers for years to come.

Printed in Great Britain
by Amazon